The Three Billy Goats Gruff

retold and illustrated by Dennis Kendrick

Random House/New York

To my mother

Library of Congress Catalog Card Number: 79-65376
ISBN: 0-394-62044-5

Manufactured in the United States of America
9 8 7 6 5 4 3 2 1

Random House Student Book Program Edition: First Printing, 1979

Once upon a time, there lived three billy goats
named Gruff.

One day, the Three Billy Goats Gruff were on their way up the mountainside to nibble the tender shoots of grass that grew near the top.

Halfway up the mountain they came to a bridge over a river. Under the bridge lived a mean and ugly troll.

The First Billy Goat Gruff began to cross the bridge.
Clip, clip! Clip, clip! went the bridge.

"Who's that clip-clipping across my bridge?" roared the troll in his meanest and ugliest voice.

"It is I, the littlest Billy Goat Gruff, and I'm on my way up the mountainside to nibble the tender shoots of grass that grow near the top."

"Oh, no you're NOT!" roared the troll. "Because I'm going to gobble you up!"

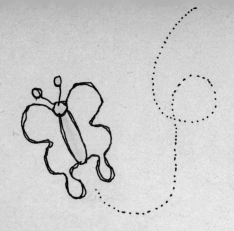

"Oh, please, Mr. Mean and Ugly Troll," pleaded the little billy goat. "Don't eat ME. Wait for the second Billy Goat Gruff to come across the bridge. He's much bigger."

"Oh, very well," snapped the troll. "You may cross —but be quick about it!"

Then the second Billy Goat Gruff
began to cross the bridge.
Clip, clop! Clip, clop!
went the bridge.

"Who's that clip-clopping across my bridge?"
roared the troll.

"It is I, the second Billy Goat Gruff, and I'm on
my way up the mountainside to nibble the tender
shoots of gr—"

"Oh, no you're NOT!" interrupted the troll.
"Because I'm going to gobble you up!"

"Don't waste your time on me," said the billy goat. "Wait for the third Billy Goat Gruff to come across the bridge. He's much bigger."

"Oh, very well," snapped the troll. "You may cross —but be quick about it!"

Then the third Billy Goat Gruff began to cross the bridge. *CLOP, CLOP! CLOP, CLOP!* went the bridge as it creaked under his weight.

"Who's that clop-clopping across my bridge?" roared the troll.

"It is I! The BIG Billy Goat Gruff!" said the billy goat in a deep voice.

"Aha!" roared the troll. "*You're* the one I'm going to gobble up!"

"That's what you think!" said the billy goat. "When I come at you with my two sharp horns, you'll have more holes in you than ten pounds of Swiss cheese!"

And with that, the billy goat flew at the troll and bashed him to bits . . .

and threw him into the river!

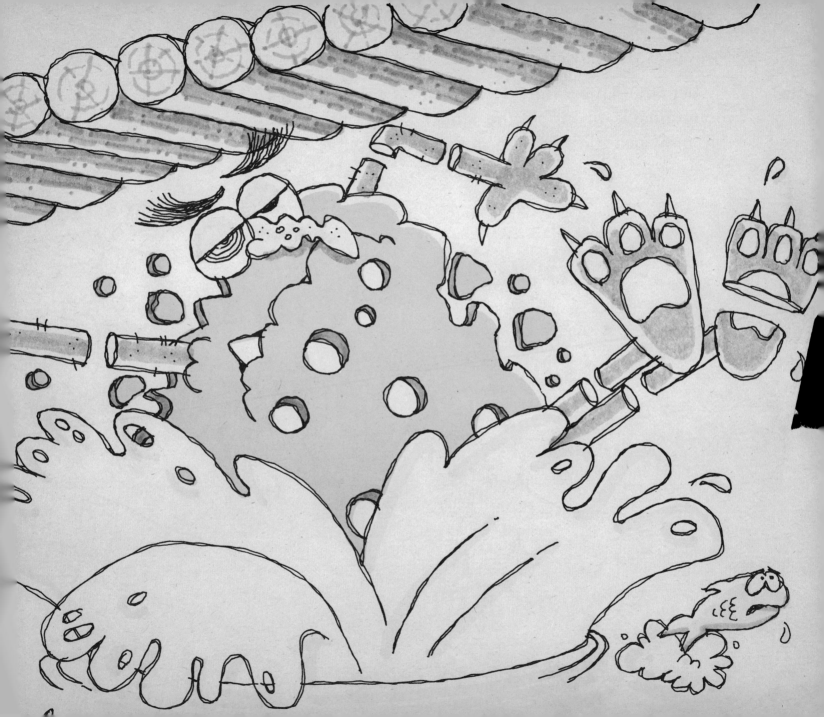

Then the Three Billy Goat Gruffs went up the mountainside to nibble the tender shoots of grass that grew near the top . . .

and they all got very, very fat indeed!